CODE NAME: CHAMELEON

Illustrated by Kim and Art Ellis

Adapted from a story by
Dean Clarrain and Steve Lavigne

Based on the Teenage Mutant Ninja Turtles
characters and comic books created by
Kevin Eastman and Peter Laird

Code Name: Chameleon created by Steve Lavigne

RANDOM HOUSE
Happy House Group

The TV news was *indeed* fascinating that night. April O'Neil had a chilling story to report.

"A police manhunt is underway for a double agent believed to have stolen top-secret weapons plans from the United Nations."

"The agent," April continued, "known by the code name *Chameleon*, gained access to the files by posing as a diplomat. The exact type of plans stolen has not been revealed. It is said, however, that they are those for a weapon more powerful than any now known to mankind."

Splinter was not the only person glued to the
television that night. Deep under the city, inside his
headquarters, the evil ninja Shredder also watched
April's report. Visions of weapons danced in his head.
"Bebop, Rocksteady!" he called to his assistants.
"I want those weapons plans and I want them *now*!"

"Uh—yeah, sure, Mister Shredder," said the mutants, laughing. "Right away."

The evil ninja took a deep breath. "I will not tolerate another failure. I want you to *find* this Chameleon and bring him to me. Take along a Foot Soldier and a Knucklehead. Use them as backups if you run into problems."

Bebop and Rocksteady hurried out into the sewer. I can't imagine what this weapon can be, thought Shredder. *But I want it!*

The crafty Chameleon, meanwhile, was busy keeping himself—along with the secret plans—from being caught. With the police hot on his trail, he ran down a dark alley.

"Halt or I'll shoot!" yelled the police officer, following him.

Chameleon didn't halt. *Ptaang!* Gunfire blasted off the alley walls.

"Time to shake these cops off my tail," Chameleon said to himself. But the alley was a dead end. There was no place to go!

Craash!

Chameleon jumped through a glass window and landed in a room filled with dressmaking dummies.

"How strange…" he said, brushing himself off. "No time to dwell on it now, however. I've got to *move*." He headed for a door marked BASEMENT.

"Ah ha!" said the double agent, checking out the basement. "A manhole. How handy!" Chameleon lifted the heavy lid and climbed down into the sewer. "Wish I hadn't worn my best tux," he said, pushing up his sleeves.

Not far away, the Teenage Mutant Ninja Turtles were patrolling the area.

"Man," said Donatello, "look at all the garbage floating in the sewer. There's a hamburger wrapper, an apple core...what might be a chocolate bar...."

"Lay off, Don. You're making me hungry!" said Michaelangelo.

But Donatello continued. "And I think that lump over there was once a plain doughnut…and there's a banana peel…and—"

"Cool it, dude. My mouth's watering!" complained Michaelangelo. He pinched the back of Donatello's leg.

"OW!" cried the turtle. "Watch that, Mikey, *or you'll make me mad!*"

"Oh, yeah?"

"*Yeah!*"

The turtles' voices carried far through the sewer. But they didn't have to go far for Chameleon to hear them. He was close by, in the very same tunnel.

"Hmmm…" he said to himself. "I think I'd better change directions."

Chameleon started climbing into the tunnel behind him.

"But…what's that?" he said. "Voices approaching from *this* direction too?"

"Uh, what's this guy s'posed to look like?" said a voice from down the tunnel.

"I'm not sure," said a second voice. "I was too busy dusting to see."

The double agent was trapped. He quickly took the stolen weapons plans and slid them into a crack in the wall. The voices were getting closer and closer. "It looks like I'm stuck in the middle..." said Chameleon, "but in the middle of *what*?"

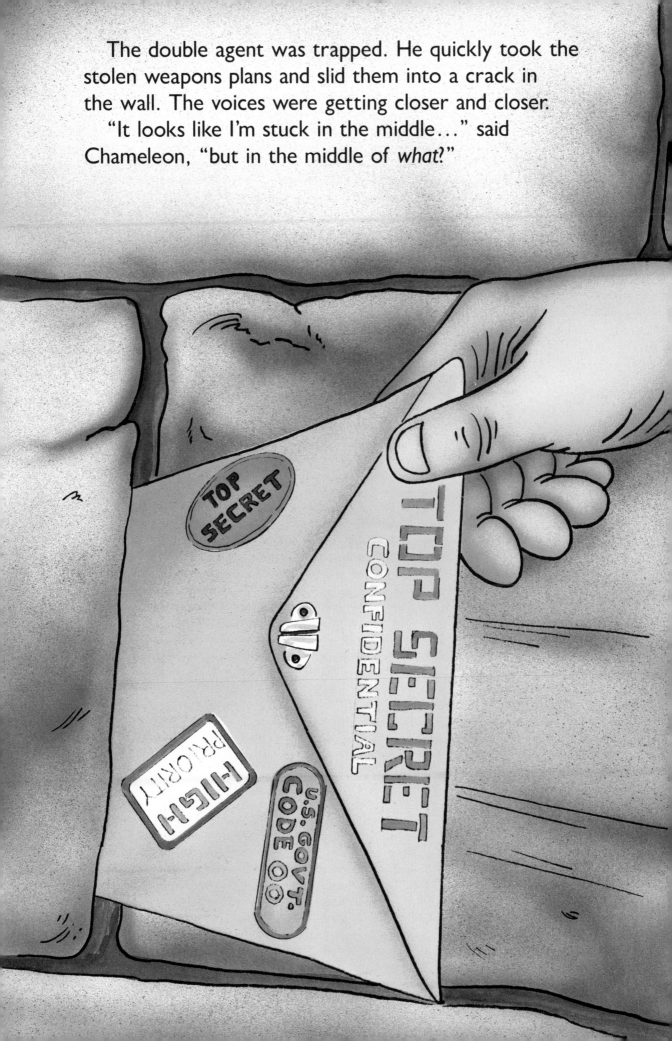

The Teenage Mutant Ninja Turtles stepped out of one tunnel. Bebop and Rocksteady stepped out of the other. "Weapons at the ready, bros!" cried Leonardo.

"You guys again!" yelled Rocksteady.

Chameleon tried to look inconspicuous. It didn't work. "Grab that guy!" Bebop said to Rocksteady. "He's the Chameleon dude!"

Rocksteady wrapped his rhino arms around Chameleon.

"I'd let go of him if I were you, Rocksteady," warned Leonardo.

"Oh, is that right," said Bebop, laughing. He gestured toward the tunnel he and Rocksteady had come from. "I'd like to *show* you something, boys. Something special."

In the tunnel a Foot Soldier sat on what looked like a giant steel spider.
"This here's a Knucklehead," Bebop continued. "Something Shredder invented for your enjoyment."

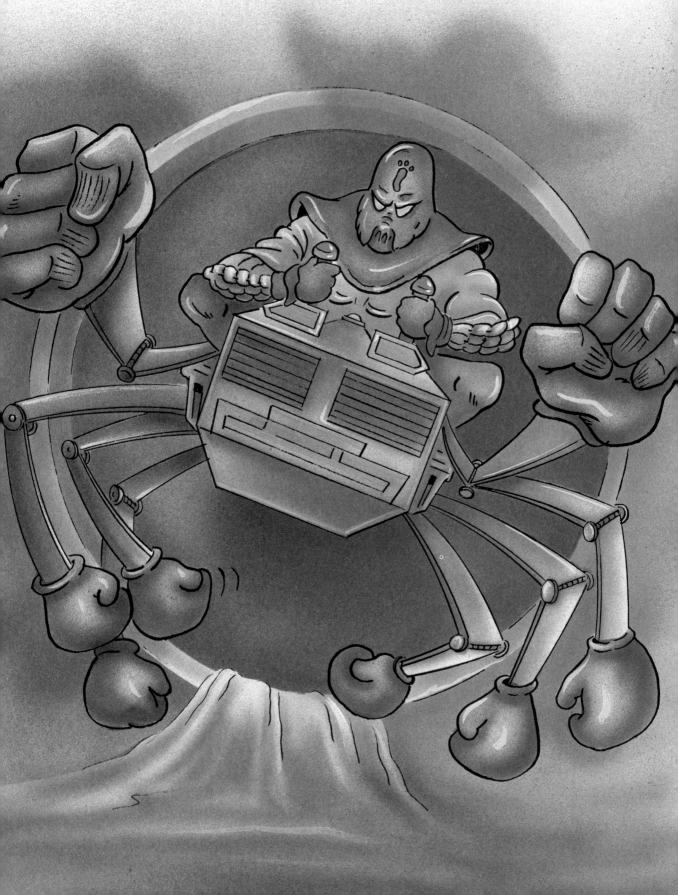

While the turtles readied themselves to fight the Knucklehead, Bebop and Rocksteady escaped down the tunnel with Chameleon.

Whack! Wham! The Knucklehead easily repelled the turtles' blows. Raphael tried knocking the Foot Soldier off the Knucklehead with a flying kick. But instead— *KLUNK!*—the turtle fell to the ground holding his foot.

"Leo—the Foot Soldier's a robot!" he groaned.

"A *robot*?" said Leonardo. "That's just what I wanted to hear!" In an instant, Leonardo had sliced the Foot Soldier in two. "See, no blood at all," he said, looking at his work. "Just a little oil."

Back at headquarters, Bebop and Rocksteady had taken Chameleon to Shredder.

"There're no weapons plans on him," said Rocksteady.

"Tie him down and bring me some mutagen," ordered Shredder.

"Can't we talk a deal?" said Chameleon.

"Certainly," answered Shredder. "You tell me where the plans are, and I'll let you live."

"I was thinking more along the lines of *selling* them to you," Chameleon said, squirming.

Shredder laughed. "I don't think you understand your *position,* fool. If you don't tell me where the plans are, I'll mutate you into a *real* chameleon-man!"

Shredder dangled a live chameleon over Chameleon.
"This isn't how I normally conduct business!" cried
the double agent.
"This isn't business," said Shredder. "This is pleasure!"
Bebop handed his boss an aerosol can of mutagen.

Shredder explained how the mutagen would turn Chameleon into a half-man, half-chameleon mutant. Then he dropped the squirming lizard onto the double agent's face. "The choice is yours," he said.

"I'm…I'm…convinced," stuttered Chameleon. He quickly told the ninja where he'd hidden the plans.

"Excellent!" said Shredder. "Bebop, Rocksteady— retrieve the plans *immediately*!"

"You can release me now, Shredder," said the double
agent.

Shredder laughed. "*Release* you? I was hoping you'd
join me." Shredder sprayed mutagen in Chameleon's
face. "But now that you're mutated, I think you'll see
things my way."

"*YOU'RE GOING TO REGRET THIS!*" screamed
Chameleon.

Suddenly Chameleon was gone!

"Huh?" said Shredder. "Where'd he go?"

Chameleon had made himself invisible. Through his mutation, he had acquired the chameleon's ability to camouflage himself. The double agent simply changed color to match the surrounding walls and made his escape.

Meanwhile, in the sewer, the turtles were just recovering from their battle with the Knucklehead. "Don't you think we've hung around here long enough?" said Raphael to his brothers. "We've got to go find Bebop and Rocksteady."

Zzap! Zap! Zap! Bebop and Rocksteady came charging into the sewer chamber, their ray guns blasting.

"Yowser!" cried Leonardo, jumping to avoid a ray. "Raph, Leo, Mike—into the tunnel! Quick!"

"There's no place to hide in there," sneered Rocksteady. He peered into the tunnel. *Whiz!* Suddenly a throwing star sliced through the air. *Whiz whiz whiz!* The mutant ran behind the Knucklehead, dodging the flying weapons. "Move it!" he yelled. "The turtles have stars!"

And so the fighting went back and forth, with the turtles throwing their stars and the mutants shooting their ray guns. Neither side was aware that the fight was being watched from above.

Camouflaged to match the ceiling, Chameleon watched the fighting below.

"It's high time to end this standoff," said Chameleon to himself. "Perhaps with a colorful and dramatic diversion?"

The sewer chamber began to glow with a bright, reddish-orange light.

"What's that?" asked Rocksteady.

"It don't matter," said Bebop. "Just shoot at it!"

Bebop and Rocksteady started shooting over their heads. Chunks of ceiling fell to the floor.

Chameleon changed color and slipped unnoticed to the ground. "I haven't forgotten my promise, Shredder!" he muttered. He slid out the stolen weapons plans from their hiding place and made his escape. He'd just stepped into the tunnel when the ceiling collapsed behind him.

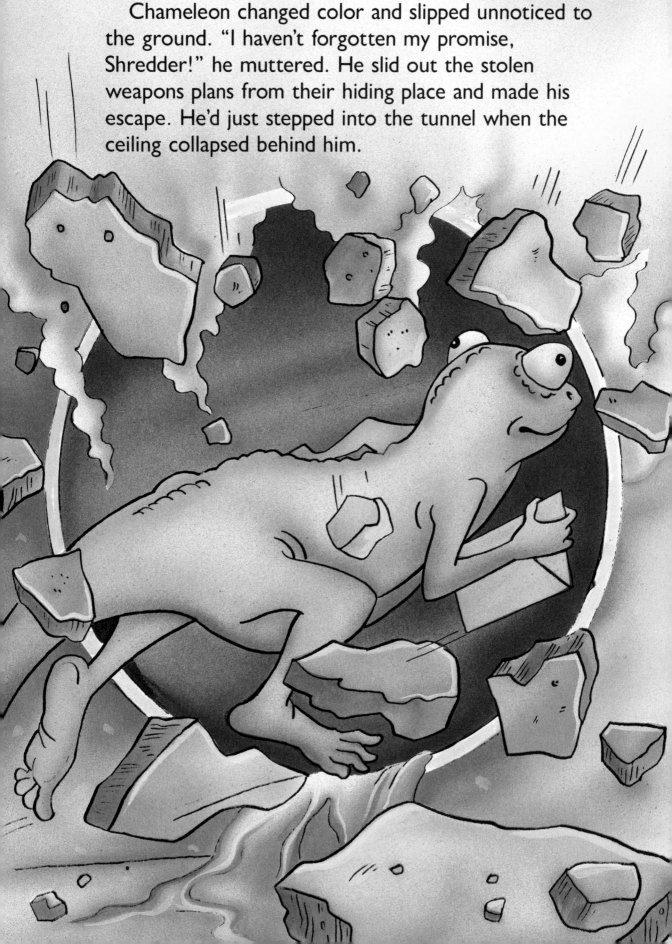

Rrruummble!

From the safety of their tunnel, the turtles watched the chamber fill with debris. "Man, we were lucky to have escaped *that!*" said Michaelangelo.

"Luckier than Bebop and Rocksteady," said Donatello. "They must be buried under a *ton* of cement."

Leonardo broke the silence. "Not much of a victory, is it?" he said.

Later that night, April O'Neil had *another* fascinating story to report.

"Secret weapons plans stolen earlier today were returned this evening. An envelope containing burned remains of the plans was found in the United Nations. It is not known *how* someone was able to pass *unseen* into the U.N. to deliver the plans, or *why* they would return the plans after they had stolen them."

But one viewer *did* know how and why the plans were returned. One viewer who'd been seeing things *a lot* differently lately.